...fierce ones, funny ones, find them all

I'm watching you!

Contents

I know what a dinosaur is! pages 4-5

Big and small pages 6-7

pages 12-13 Dinner time!

pages 14-15 Killer instinct

The dinosaurs were the biggest *land* animals ever...

Dinosaur detectives

We know about dinosaurs because we have found fossils of their **bones** and fitted them together.

fossils

Dinosaur bones harden into rock over millions of years—these are called fossils. Dinosaur detectives have found fossils of bones, claws, teeth, eggs, footprints, and even dinosaur poop. The detectives fit the bones together like a jigsaw puzzle to make a dinosaur.

What am I? These sharp-looking rocks used to be huge dinosaur teeth.

What am I? This oval rock is actually a fossilized dinosaur egg.

What am I? Watch where you step! This rock has a dinosaur footprint in it.

What am I? Look out, don't step on it! These rocks are dinosaur poop!

Fossilized dino poop can show what dinosaurs ate.

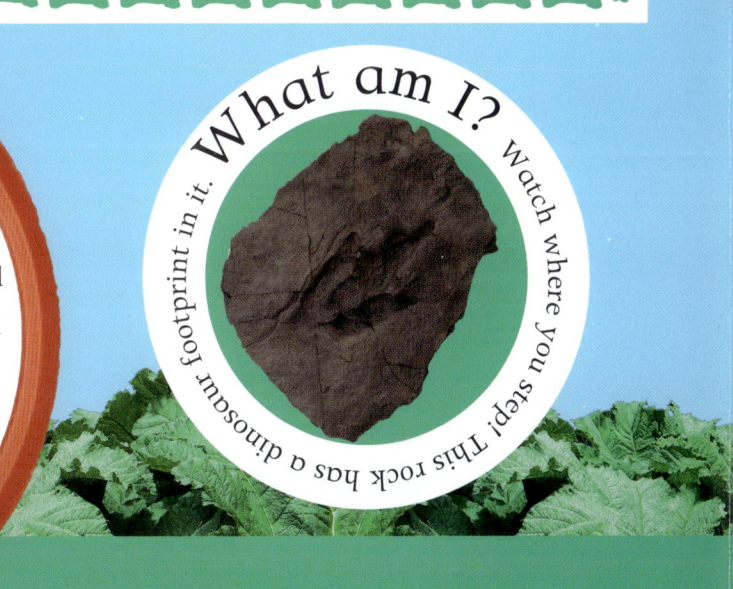

Dinosaur detectives are called paleontologists.

Dinosaur fossils are found all over the world.

Eggs, eggs, eggs pages **8-9**

Weird, wonderful, and colorful! pages **10-11**

pages **18-19** **Sky high, Ocean deep**

pages **16-17** **Danger!**

No dinosaurs could fly. There were flying creatures that looked like dinosaurs but they were actually flying reptiles. They lived at the same time as the dinosaurs.

...but the blue whale is the biggest animal of all time.

I know what a dinosaur is!

Dinosaurs walked on either two or four legs

Millions of years ago there were no people, no houses, and no cars. Instead, our world was ruled by the **biggest** land animals ever—the dinosaurs.

About 500 different kinds of dinosaur have been found.

Tyrannosaurus had the biggest teeth

birds

Dinobirds
Some dinosaur detectives think that birds are the closest relatives to dinosaurs because some dinosaurs have been found with feathers.

Why can't we see dinosaurs today?
No one really knows why there are no dinosaurs around today. Some people think an enormous rock crashed into Earth from outer space and caused them to die out.

crash!

Rocks from space are called meteors

The first dinosaur bone was found 300 years ago.

The biggest footprint ever found was so big it could hold as much water as a bathtub!

Dinosaurs

Dinosaurs looked a little like reptiles, such as crocodiles, but they walked with their legs straight underneath them. This made them much faster.

Open the flap to find dino relatives

Dino-pals

Some of the animals we see today were around with the dinosaurs millions of years ago. Crocodiles were here before dinosaurs!

"We were here before you Mr. Dinosaur!"

G**iganotosauru**s

Dinosaurs lived for 160 million years, but disappeared 65 million years ago.

Big and small

Dinosaurs were the **biggest** animals ever to have walked the land—far bigger than any animals we can see today.

Monster-dino

The biggest dinosaur ever was called the *Sauroposeidon*. It was longer than four buses.

Dinosaur means "terrible lizard" in Greek—but they weren't really lizards at all.

Egg-painting

No one knows exactly what color dinosaur eggs were, so paint chicken eggs the color you imagine they were.

Step one
Ask an adult to hard-boil your chicken eggs so that they won't break easily.

Step two
Use acrylic paints to decorate them when they are cool enough to hold.

Step three
Leave them to dry. Take photographs, because you'll have to throw them away after a few days.

make it scary

make it sweet

eek, what's inside?

Stripes, spots, lines, or dots?

Dinosaurs laid **eggs**, just like reptiles and birds. Some made nests, too.

A Maiasaura's nest was as big as

We know dinosaurs laid eggs because...

sauropods
The largest dinosaurs were the sauropods. They were the biggest land animals ever to walk the Earth.

tyrannosaurus
Tyrannosaurus rex was one of the most ferocious dinosaurs, but even he looks small compared to the sauropods.

stegosaurus
Stegosaurus was bigger than an elephant and had spiked plates as big as kites.

elephant
The bull elephant is the biggest land animal you can see today.

child
This is how big you would be compared to the dinosaurs.

compsognathus
The *Compsognathus* was the size of a chicken.

These dinos were taller than trees!

The *Compsognathus* is one of the smallest dinosaurs that has been found yet.

Eggs, eggs, eggs

Biggest egg
The biggest egg ever found belonged to the *Hypselosaurus*. The egg was about as long as from your elbow to your fingertips. Other eggs were small enough to fit in your hand.

Dinosaur nests

Many dinosaurs built nests, like this *Maiasaura*, which made nests of mud to lay her eggs in.

paddling pool!

Mother care

Some dinosaurs looked after their babies, like birds do today. They fed them until they could care for themselves.

hello mommy!

...fossils of nests full of eggs have been found.

Barosaurus

Pentaceratops

Weird,

Parasaurolophus

Stegosaurus

...and colorful!

Dinosaurs came in all kinds of weird shapes. Some had horns, others had head **crests**, and some had very strange **lumps** and bumps.

corythosaurus

caudipteryx

But what color were they?

Nobody knows what color dinosaurs were because we only have their bones to tell us about them. Lots of people try to guess what colors they were, based on animals alive today.

Now draw your own...

What do you think? Were they brown or blue, striped or spotted?

Step 1 Draw your favorite dinosaur on a piece of paper.

Step 2 Color it in, cut it out, and put it on your wall.

...or mold your own

Use modeling clay to mold your own colorful dinosaur.

purple

pink

green

bones

modeling clay

Pteranodon

Therizinosaurus

wonderful...

Plateosaurus

Troodon

Dinner time!

Menu—meat eaters

◆ Watch out! A *Tyrannosaurus* could gobble you up in one big gulp!

◆ *Triceratops'* bones have been found in *Tyrannosaurus's* tummy.

look at the size of those teeth!

Tyrannosaurus rex had teeth as long as a man's foot—that's big!

Suchomimus

fishy diet

Suchomimus was as big as *Tyrannosaurus rex*, but it lived near water and ate fish. It had up to 100 razor-sharp teeth.

Suchomimus probably used its huge thumb claws as hooks to catch fish.

Teeth

Dinosaurs had lots of different types of teeth that were perfect for tearing, chewing, or cracking open their favorite food.

Sharp teeth
Giganotosaurus had masses of enormous, sharp teeth to tear up meat.

Front teeth
Barosaurus had teeth at the front of its jaws to grab plant bunches.

No teeth
Oviraptor had a toothless beak, which it may have used to crack eggs.

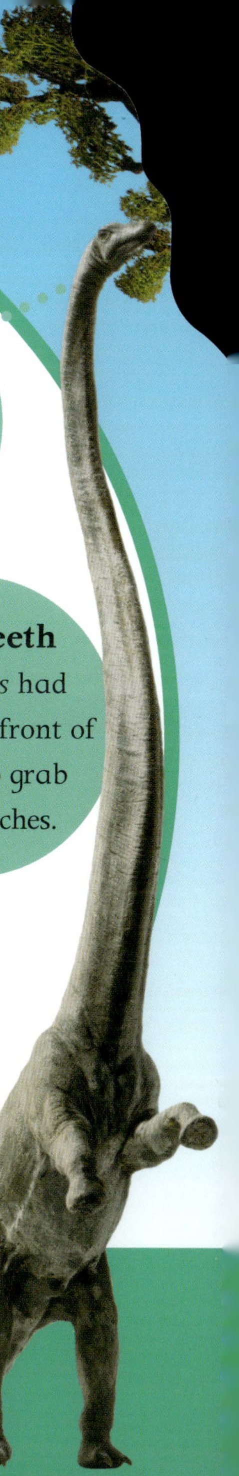

Tough teeth
Tricerotops had a beak to tear tough plants, and cheek teeth to chew them.

Dinosaur diets

The dinosaur world was divided into gentle plant eaters and **ferocious** meat eaters. What's on the menu?

Menu—vegetarians

- The sauropods could eat 400 lbs (200 kg) of conifers and ferns per day.
- They would eat a handful of stones to help grind up food. 

Killer instinct

Small dinosaurs were some of the most **vicious** meat-eaters. They ganged up in **packs** to attack bigger dinosaurs.

Stick together
Many dinosaurs, like this *Pachyrhinosaurus*, stuck together in large groups to keep safe.

We can tell what a dinosaur ate by looking at the bones in its poop!

Velociraptor had very muscular legs, which it used to jump on its prey.

Gallimimus

Gallimimus is thought to have been the fastest dinosaur and would run to escape meat-eaters like *Velociraptor*. It could run as fast as a racehorse.

velociraptor

These dinosaurs had teeth like knives, and fingers and toes armed with daggerlike claws. They attacked big dinosaurs in packs.

watch out

here we come!

don't eat me!

15

Danger!

With such terrifying meat-eaters as this *Tyrannosaurus* around, dinosaurs had to be **careful** not to get caught. Big dinosaurs were slow so they had to find other ways to fight.

Whipping tail
The big sauropods, like this *Barosaurus*, had tails as long as their bodies. If attacked, they could lash out at enemies.

Many dinos were too big to hide.

Sharp horns

Tricerotops had three horns on its face and a frill made of bone to protect its neck. Its horns could grow to the size of a man's arm.

Suit of armor

Stegosaurus had thick armorlike skin, spines along its tail, and big plates all along its back to protect itself.

watch that thumb!

Club tail

Euoplocephalus had a club at the end of its tail that it probably used to swing around and thump an enemy.

Thumbs up!

This *Iguanodon* had a spiked thumb on each hand. It used them to stab other animals if it felt threatened.

Stegosaurus was about the length of a big truck.

Dinosaurs all had thick skin.

thumb

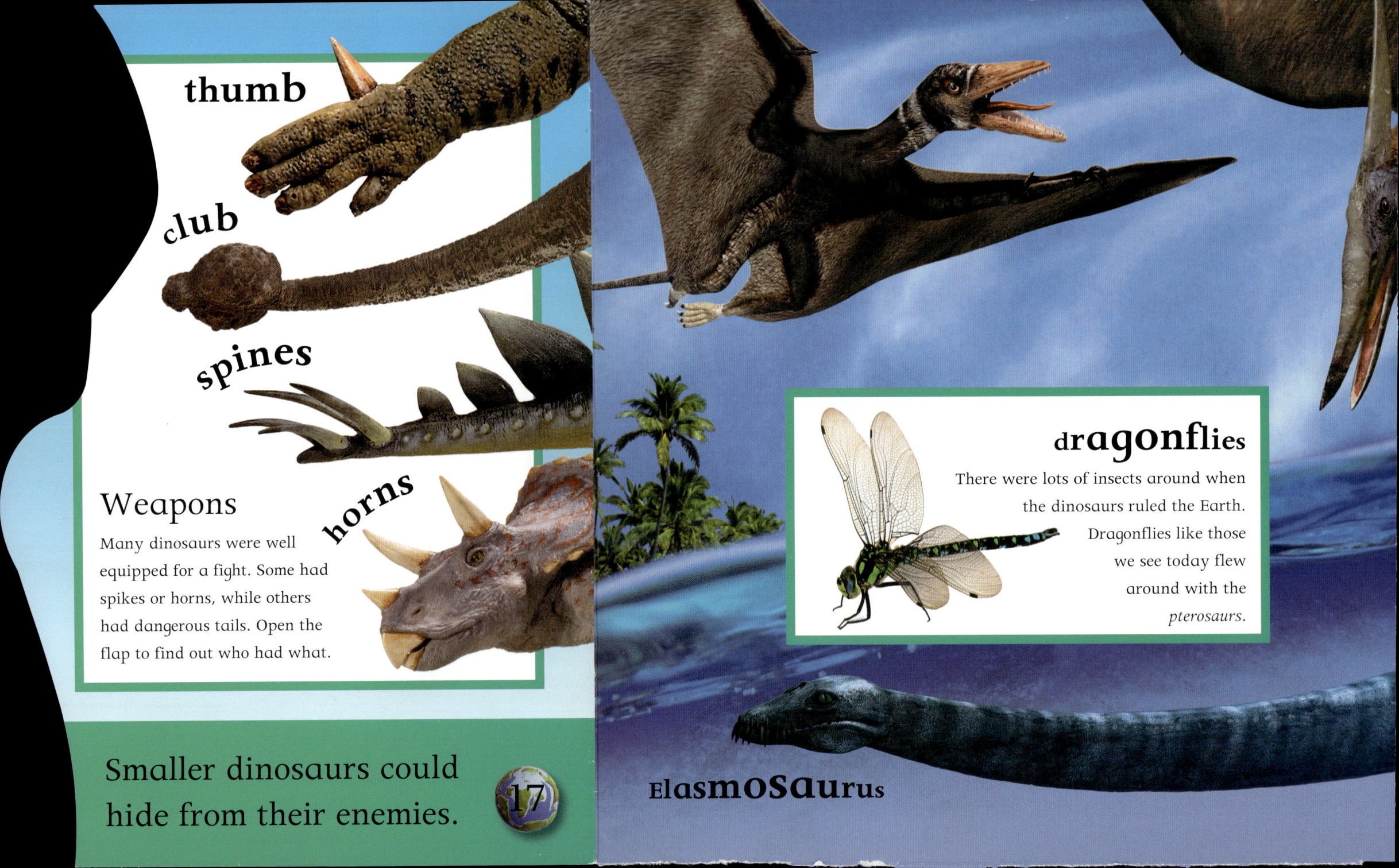

club

spines

Weapons

horns

Many dinosaurs were well equipped for a fight. Some had spikes or horns, while others had dangerous tails. Open the flap to find out who had what.

Smaller dinosaurs could hide from their enemies.

17

dragonflies

There were lots of insects around when the dinosaurs ruled the Earth. Dragonflies like those we see today flew around with the *pterosaurs*.

Elasmosaurus

Dimorphodon

Sky high

Dinosaurs couldn't fly, but there were other animals that lived in the skies at the same time. Flying reptiles, called **pterosaurs**, and insects ruled the skies.

sea serpent

The *Elasmosaurus* was a huge sea reptile that grew to 46 ft (14 m)—that's as long as five small cars! Its neck took up half its body length.

ichthyosaurus

the sea was full of fish, crabs, and jellyfish, too

Ocean deep

At the time of the dinosaurs the sea was filled with many strange **creatures**, but also some animals you would recognize today, such as this shark.

sharks have been around for millions of years

fish-eaters

Many *pterosaurs* had long beaks filled with lots of teeth. They probably flew just above the water scooping up fish in their beaks.

data

dinosaur name	how do you say it?	what does it mean?
pachyrhinosaurus	PACK-ee-RYE-no-SORE-us	thick-nosed lizard
pterosaur	TER-oh-sore	winged lizard
sauropod	SAW-roh-pod	lizard-hipped
sauroposeidon	SAW-roh-poh-SI-don	lizard poseidon
stegosaurus	steg-oh-SORE-us	plated lizard
suchomimus	SUE-koh-MIME-uss	crocodile mimic
triceratops	try-SERRA-tops	three-horned face
tyrannosaurus	tie-RAN-o-SORE-uss	tyrant lizard
velociraptor	vell-OSS-ee-RAP-tor	swift robber

pterosaurs

Pterosaurs were huge flying reptiles. They looked more like bats than birds, with their leathery wings and hairy bodies.

Quetzalcoatlus was as big as a two-seater airplane!

quetzalcoatlus

sordes

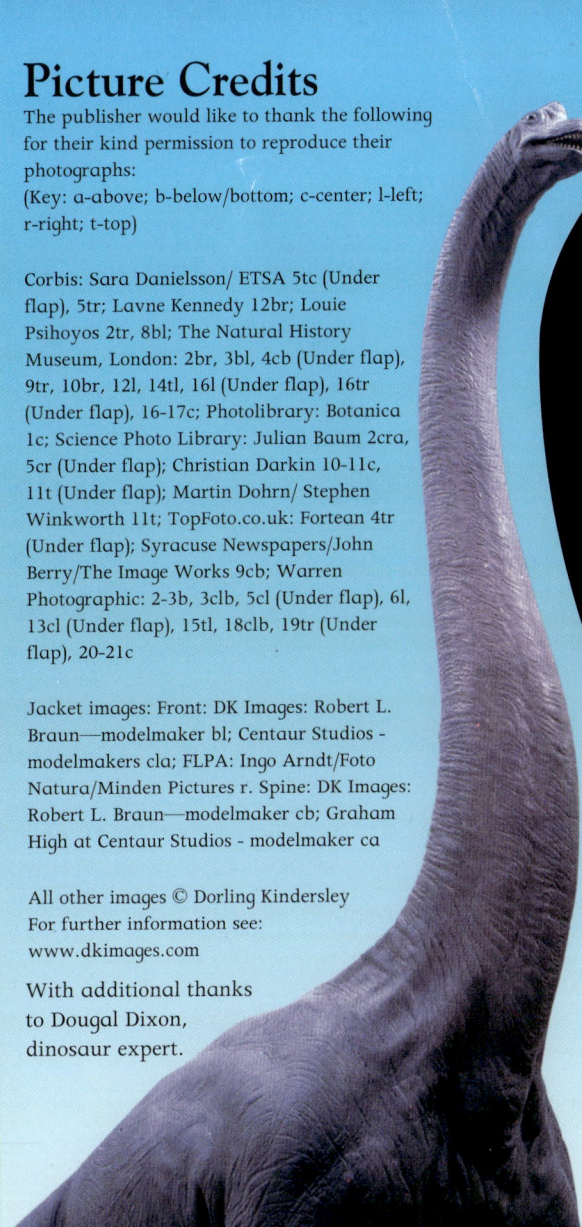

LONDON, NEW YORK, MUNICH,
MELBOURNE, and DELHI

Written by
Penelope Arlon

Designed by
Cathy Chesson

Production Editor: Hitesh Patel
Publishing Manager: Sue Leonard
Art Director: Rachael Foster
US Editor: Margaret Parrish

First published in the United States in 2008 by
DK Publishing
375 Hudson Street
New York, New York 10014

08 09 10 11 12 10 9 8 7 6 5 4 3 2 1
Copyright © 2008 Dorling Kindersley Ltd.

All rights reserved under International and Pan-American Copyright Conventions. No part of this publication may be reproduced, stored in a retrieval system, or transmitted in any form or by any means electronic, mechanical, photocopying, recording, or otherwise, without prior written permission of the copyright owner. Published in Great Britain by Dorling Kindersley Limited.

A catalog record for this book is available from the Library of Congress.

ISBN: 978-0-7566-3439-1

Color reproduction by MDP, UK
Printed and bound in China by
Hung Hing Off-set Printing Co., Ltd.

Discover more at
www.dk.com

Picture Credits

The publisher would like to thank the following for their kind permission to reproduce their photographs:
(Key: a-above; b-below/bottom; c-center; l-left; r-right; t-top)

Corbis: Sara Danielsson/ ETSA 5tc (Under flap), 5tr; Lavne Kennedy 12br; Louie Psihoyos 2tr, 8bl; The Natural History Museum, London: 2br, 3bl, 4cb (Under flap), 9tr, 10br, 12l, 14tl, 16l (Under flap), 16tr (Under flap), 16-17c; Photolibrary: Botanica 1c; Science Photo Library: Julian Baum 2cra, 5cr (Under flap); Christian Darkin 10-11c, 11t (Under flap); Martin Dohrn/ Stephen Winkworth 11t; TopFoto.co.uk: Fortean 4tr (Under flap); Syracuse Newspapers/John Berry/The Image Works 9cb; Warren Photographic: 2-3b, 3clb, 5cl (Under flap), 6l, 13cl (Under flap), 15tl, 18clb, 19tr (Under flap), 20-21c

Jacket images: Front: DK Images: Robert L. Braun—modelmaker bl; Centaur Studios - modelmakers cla; FLPA: Ingo Arndt/Foto Natura/Minden Pictures r. Spine: DK Images: Robert L. Braun—modelmaker cb; Graham High at Centaur Studios - modelmaker ca

All other images © Dorling Kindersley
For further information see:
www.dkimages.com

With additional thanks to Dougal Dixon, dinosaur expert.

dinosaur

dinosaur name	how do you say it?	what does it mean?
compsognathus	komp-sog-NAY-thus	pretty jaw
barosaurus	barrow-SORE-uss	heavy lizard
elasmosaurus	ee-LAZ-moe-SORE-uss	plate lizard
euoplocephalus	YOU-owe-ploh-SEFF-a-luss	well-armored head
gallimimus	gally-MEEM-uss	chicken mimic
giganotosaurus	jig-anno-toe-SORE-uss	giant lizard
iguanodon	ig-WAHN-o-don	iguana tooth
maiasaura	MY-a-SORE-a	good mother lizard
oviraptor	oh-vee-RAP-tor	egg robber